BEETROOT GIRL

ELT GRADED READER—CEFR LEVEL A2-B1

TIMOTHY BURTON

All characters and situations in this publication are fictitious, and any resemblance to living persons is purely coincidental.

Beetroot Girl, by Timothy Burton

Cover design by Samantha Burton
Cover and interior illustrations courtesy of www.shutterstock.com and www.pixabay.com

Melissa turned bright red.

Red as a beetroot.

Red as a tomato.

It wasn't her fault. She always went red when people stared at her. However, today it was worse.

Today was her first day at a new school.

Life isn't easy for Melissa when she moves to Brighton. She's deep-thinking and independent, but blushes easily—something that draws the attention of bullies.

Join her as she tries to overcome the bullying and emerge victorious.

Inspiring and relatable, BEETROOT GIRL is an easy reader for English language learners. It's designed for strong elementary to pre-intermediate learners: Common European Framework of Reference for Languages (CEFR) A2-B1 level, with pre-reading vocabulary exercises and comprehension and discussion questions after each chapter.

To Richard, Vicky, Tyler and Iris.
Looking forward to catching up again.

How to use this book

This easy reader is designed for strong elementary to pre-intermediate learners: Common European Framework of Reference for Languages (CEFR) A2-B1 level.

Students should complete the vocabulary pre-reading exercise at the beginning of each chapter before continuing. These exercises are essential for building vocabulary and making comprehension easier.

In addition, there are comprehension and discussion questions to complete at the end of each chapter.

Chapter One: First Day Nightmare

PRE-READING VOCABULARY EXERCISE

Match the words (1-13) with their definitions (a-m):

1. beetroot	a. become red in the face
2. delight	b. selected as aim for attack
3. blushing	c. hit with the foot
4. to make fun	d. unseen, hidden
5. inconspicuous	e. terrible
6. snorted	f. behave as if something is the case when it is not
7. hunched	g. dark-red vegetable
8. target	h. an arrogant, unpleasant smile
9. kicking	i. lose self-control
10. awful	j. great pleasure
11. snapped	k. make jokes about
12. smirking	l. make explosive sound through nose
13. pretended	m. raise shoulders and bend forward

CHAPTER SUMMARY

It's Melissa's first day at her new school. She blushes very easily, and the other students tease her. The teacher asks another student a question, and he is unable to answer. The students tease him too. Melissa feels sorry for him but does not help him.

Melissa turned bright red.

Red as a beetroot.

Red as a tomato.

It wasn't her fault. She always went red when people stared at her. However, today it was worse.

Today was her first day at a new school.

"What colour's red?" called out someone from the back of the classroom.

"Looks like we've got beetroot on the menu for lunch today," shouted out a girl to Melissa's left, to the delight of the other students.

Everyone laughed.

Melissa's face grew hotter and hotter. She couldn't stop blushing.

"That's enough, everyone," said Ms Hughes, her new mathematics teacher. "I simply asked you to make Melissa feel welcome at our school, *not* to make fun of her."

The class went quiet then, and Melissa's face started to slowly cool.

"Since you're all so full of energy, let's get straight to work," continued the teacher. "Please open your new textbooks and turn to page fifteen." Ms Hughes began walking about the room. "Let's see what you can remember from last term, shall we?"

Groans went up from around the room.

Melissa kept her head down, trying to remain inconspicuous. She didn't want to be asked a question.

She bent down then and pulled her textbook from her bag. She placed it down on her desk and stared at it, to avoid catching the teacher's eye. 'Fun with Maths' was the name of the book. Melissa snorted to herself. *Whatever is fun about maths? They must think we are idiots.*

She heard the teacher put her first question to another student. *Phew!*

Actually, Melissa *really* didn't enjoy maths.

Her dad certainly possessed great skill with numbers. In fact, he was a lecturer in mathematics. He was now a professor at Brighton University. But, unlike him, Melissa had very little ability.

She opened the book at the correct place and began to read:

A meat pie costs c pence and a packet of crisps costs d pence. Write down an expression for the cost of 2 meat pies and 2 packets of crisps.

The room went quiet again. The teacher was looking for the next student to ask a question. *Don't ask me. Don't ask me,* she thought.

"Melissa, can you do this one for us, please?"

She hunched further over her desk.

"Ummm ... $1c + 2d$?" Melissa replied hesitantly, suddenly feeling warm again.

"Speak English," said a boy to Melissa's right. "We can't hear you."

"Good try, Melissa," said the teacher, ignoring the boy. "Close ... can anyone help her, please?"

"$2c + 2d$, Ms Hughes?" said the student behind her.

"Well done, Noah."

The teacher walked past Melissa then, as she made her way to the back of the class, in search of her next 'target'. Melissa sighed. She should be safe for a while now at least.

Then Noah began kicking the back of her chair.

Thump. Thump. Thump.

Anger rose inside her, the blood pumping through her ears.

She didn't want to be here. She felt completely alone. Her best friend, Hannah, lived in Birmingham, and her parents didn't seem to care about her happiness.

Thump. Thump. Thump.

I'm going to text Hannah and tell her just how awful this new school is, she thought.

She was about to turn around to tell Noah to stop kicking her chair, when he suddenly stopped.

The room went silent. Melissa turned to see everyone was looking at a boy. He had untidy hair and wore a blue school jumper that was much too big for him. He stared down at the page while Ms Hughes stood over him, waiting for the answer to her latest question.

"Come on, please, Andy," said Ms Hughes. "Do your best."

He didn't answer.

Melissa found it difficult to watch. But she was fascinated, too. She hated to admit it, but she was actually relieved that, at least, it wasn't *her* in difficulty now.

"Yeah, come on Andy Pandy," a student shouted out from the back of the class.

"That's enough, Liam," snapped the teacher.

Liam grinned but remained silent.

"But we haven't got all day," said the student beside Liam.

"Yeah, Ms Hughes," called out a girl from the other side of the room. "James has to be in bed by seven." Many students laughed at this – but Melissa tensed.

"Quiet, please, Kylie," said the teacher, frowning. "Okay, Liam ... and James," she said to the two trouble-makers. "Come and see me after class." Ms Hughes turned to another boy sitting with them. "Josh ... perhaps you can answer the question for us?"

Melissa noticed how cute Josh was. However, she didn't like his smirking friends.

"Ummm ... $4x = 3$?"

"Correct, Josh."

Melissa turned back to her maths book and pretended to study it again. She looked at the next exercise and frowned. She didn't know the answer to that one either.

Maybe her day would improve once maths class was over.

But then Noah started kicking the back of her chair again. "Hey, Beetroot Girl," he whispered. "What colour's red?"

COMPREHENSION QUESTIONS

1. Why does Melissa try to avoid making eye contact with the teacher?

2. What does Noah do that really annoys Melissa?

3. How does the teacher punish Liam and James?

DISCUSSION QUESTIONS

1. Melissa blushes easily because she is embarrassed. Do you blush easily? What embarrasses you?

2. Melissa sees the other students bullying Andy. Rather than help him, she is just relieved they are not bullying her. What would you do in this situation, if you were Melissa?

Chapter Two: New Friends

PRE-READING VOCABULARY EXERCISE

Match the words (1-22) with their definitions (a-v):

1. piled	a. pull someone along forcefully
2. unpack	b. screw up into a ball
3. stern	c. eggs beaten and then cooked by stirring gently
4. harsh	d. pulled
5. crusts	e. bend one's head and body in fear
6. moping	f. shut forcefully
7. punched	g. stop talking (rude)
8. headlock	h. bully/victimise someone
9. dragged	i. open and remove what is inside
10. scrambled eggs	j. serious, frowning
11. picking on	k. paved public walk along the seafront
12. yanked	l. something that smells bad
13. slamming	m. frightening
14. swiping on	n. severe, unpleasantly rough
15. cringed	o. place things on top of each other
16. Brummie	p. fried cake in the shape of a ring
17. scrunched up	q. hit with the fist
18. stinky	r. slang term for a person from Birmingham
19. promenade	s. sitting around feeling unhappy
20. donut	t. to hold your arm firmly around someone's head
21. scary	u. pass a card over an electronic device
22. shut up	v. outer part of a loaf of bread

CHAPTER SUMMARY

It's the next day, and Melissa is unhappy about returning to school because of the bullying. Her father is unsympathetic and gives her questionable advice. Her mother offers to contact the school about the bullying. On the way to school, other students bully her on the bus. Melissa also makes friends with two girls from her class.

"I don't want to go back to school."

"Melissa, please," her dad replied. "I don't have time for this."

It was messy in the kitchen. All around them were boxes of their belongings, piled high. This was a new house, and they still had to properly unpack.

Melissa's dad gave her a stern look from across the breakfast table. "You know, Melissa, sometimes in life, we all have to do things we don't want to do."

"That's a bit harsh, John," her mother replied. "Try and be a little more sympathetic towards your daughter." She turned to Melissa then. "Mel, you've only been there one day. I know you miss Hannah, and I understand that you were happy back in Birmingham. But you have to at least give Brighton a try. Why don't you go down and explore the seafront with Misty sometime? Take her for a swim."

Melissa nodded. She looked at Misty then. Her shaggy dog sat near the table, waiting patiently for crusts of buttered toast.

"I was bullied at school, too, you know," her dad spoke up again. "It's not like you're special. But there is no point moping about it. You need to learn to defend yourself. James Barclay once punched me in the stomach, so I grabbed him in a headlock and dragged him around the school grounds, before punch—"

“Okay, John, that’s enough,” her mum interrupted him. She was busy at the stove now, stirring scrambled eggs. “We don’t want to encourage violence. The thing is, Mel, you have to remember that many bullied children have difficult pasts. Unhappy family lives – parents who don’t love them. They’re not as lucky as you.”

She carried the eggs over to the table and poured them onto their plates. “Just give it a chance. Sooner or later, they’ll get bored and start bullying someone else.”

Melissa remembered her relief the previous day in class when they started picking on Andy instead of her. The fact that another kid suffered instead of her didn’t seem like much of a recommendation for school either.

“Look ... if you want, your dad and I can talk to the school principal,” her mum continued. “Would you like that?”

Melissa thought seriously about it before shaking her head. Maybe her mother was right. She was new to Brighton. Perhaps Day Two would be better. “Thanks, mum,” she replied, “but I’ll see how it goes for a bit.”

“Well, just let me know,” her mum replied. “Now, finish your toast and eggs, or you’ll be late for school.”

Melissa ate her scrambled eggs and gave a crust of toast to Misty. She then left the table and grabbed her bag.

Misty followed her towards the door.

“Sorry, Misty. You know you can’t come to school with me. But trust me – it’s not much fun anyway.” She bent down then to shake the dog’s paw goodbye. “I promise to take you out for a run when I get home.”

And with that, she yanked the door open and headed off to catch the bus, slamming the door behind her.

Melissa caught the bus just in time. After swiping on with her card, she took a seat by the window and gazed out as they travelled down the hill.

"Hey, look, it's Beetroot Girl."
Melissa cringed.
She couldn't believe her bad luck. She hadn't noticed Liam and James from school sitting just behind her.
"What's that smell?" said Liam.
"It's probably your socks," laughed James.
"Nah ... it's the dirty Brummie over there."
A ball of scrunched up paper then hit Melissa on the head.
"What colour's red, stinky?"
Melissa rose from her seat and moved towards the front of the bus, as they continued to shout insults after her. Her face was hot now, and she just wanted to find somewhere away from those kids.
Day Two has got off to a good start. Not.
She was nearing the front of the bus, when a girl waved to her. Melissa recognised her, and the girl sitting beside her, from school.
"Hey Melissa, you can sit with us, if you like?"
Melissa smiled. She sat down behind the girls, next to an elderly woman with shopping bags at her feet.
"We're in the same class," the girl said. "You've seen us, right? I'm Jade, and this is Amira."
"Hi. You're new to Brighton, aren't you?" asked Amira.
Melissa couldn't believe it. These two were actually being nice to her? "Yeah, we moved down from Birmingham last week."
"Do you like it here?" asked Jade.
Melissa shrugged. "I haven't looked around properly yet." Actually, she hated Brighton so far, but she didn't want to be rude about the place to her new friends.
"It's great down by the sea," said Amira. "You can walk along the promenade, go swimming ... shopping ... and then there's the *Brighton Pole*."
Jade grinned. "Yeah. It's a tall viewing platform that's shaped like a donut."
The three chatted together as the bus made the journey towards school.
"Most of the teachers are nice," Jade told her, "but watch out for Mrs Munro."

Amira nodded. "Yeah, she's scary and marks really hard."
"It's not the teachers that worry me," Melissa admitted.
Jade frowned. "Most of the students are okay, you just have to—"
The brakes squealed then as the bus pulled up at the stop just outside the school, and the students from Beal High disembarked.
Melissa, Jade, and Amira made their way inside. Ahead, a group of boys were kicking a ball around. One of them was Josh, the cute boy from class. He saw Melissa watching him, and he smiled.
Face hot, Melissa looked away.
"Don't worry about the bullies," Amira said then. "They're just immature."
Melissa smiled back. However, her stomach tensed when Liam and James walked past.
"Hey, Beetroot Girl," Liam called out. He then grinned at James. "Look, she's—"
"Shut up, Liam," Amira snapped.

COMPREHENSION QUESTIONS

1. What does Melissa's mother suggest she does to get to know Brighton better?

2. What promise does Melissa make to her dog, Misty?

3. Why did Melissa move towards the front of the bus?

DISCUSSION QUESTIONS

1. Melissa's father talks about how bullying was dealt with in the past. He entered into a physical fight with his bully. Do you think this is a good idea? Why or why not?

2. Melissa's mum offers to go into school to talk to the principal about the bullying problem. Melissa declines

the offer. Would you get help from the school in the same situation? Why or why not?

3. Melissa makes two new friends, Jade and Amira. Is finding new friends a good way to combat bullying? Why or why not?

Chapter Three: A Day in the Sun

PRE-READING VOCABULARY EXERCISE

Match the words (1-11) with their definitions (a-k):

1. survived	a. happy
2. leaped	b. rise sharply
3. cheerful	c. very beautiful
4. mumbled	d. indicate something isn't to be taken seriously
5. steep	e. move rapidly from side to side
6. peered	f. continue to live
7. gorgeous	g. person who is unsuccessful in life
8. wagging	h. look with concentration
9. just kidding	i. move and jump quickly and suddenly
10. losers	j. spend time with
11. hanging around	k. speak so it is difficult for others to hear

CHAPTER SUMMARY

Jade and Amira invite Melissa to the beach. She and her dog, Misty, walk down to the town. Melissa thinks she sees a boy from school she likes, but it wasn't him. She notices a poster for a fun run and suggests the three friends enter. The other two are not enthusiastic. After a great day out, they see Andy from school. He wants to spend time with them, but her friends want to escape him. Later, they are rude about him.

Text message: Off 2 beach 2day. Wanna come? Jade and Amira.

Saturday. Melissa survived the first week at her new school, but it wasn't easy.

Someone pushed her in the corridor on Tuesday.

On Wednesday, a boy threw her books across the classroom.

The following lunchtime, a group of girls called out "Beetroot Girl" in the dinner hall when she walked by. And then they all laughed.

But at least now she wouldn't have to go back for two whole days. And she had new friends. She was excited to get their invitation and texted back immediately. She could walk down with Misty and join them on the promenade.

After arranging to meet at the bottom of the *Brighton Pole* at 11am (Jade had assured her she couldn't miss it), Melissa leaped out of bed and went down for breakfast. Misty was already there, as usual, waiting for any toast crumbs.

"Sorry, Misty." She patted the dog's head. "No run today. We'll have to go tomorrow instead. I'll take you down to the seafront with me though."

Melissa wasn't particularly sporty, but she loved running. It helped clear her head, and she always took Misty with her. There was a running club at her new school, but she'd never join. She went cold at the very idea. *They'd just bully me there too*, she thought.

"Good to see you up early, Melissa," said her dad. "You look cheerful this morning?"

"I'm going down to the seafront to meet Jade and Amira," she mumbled.

Across the kitchen, her mum smiled. "What a nice idea. I knew you'd make new friends soon. Do you want bacon and eggs on toast? Just don't give any of it to that dog. Misty – out of the kitchen, now!"

The sun was shining as Melissa and Misty headed down into town. The way was steep, and she wasn't looking forward to walking back up, but Misty didn't seem to care. The dog was always keen to go out.

For the first time all week, Melissa felt truly relaxed and free. *I can't wait till I can leave school, and then I can do what I want,* she thought.

Reaching the High Street, she stopped and peered into a number of clothing shops as she made her way down to the promenade. A pair of blue Nike trainers in a sports store really caught her eye.

Outside *Brighton Books,* someone had left a bowl of water for any passing dogs. Misty took a drink, before the pair continued down onto the promenade and along to the base of the Brighton Pole.

Jade had said she couldn't miss it, and she was right. It was visible from miles around.

Her friends were already there.

"Sorry, I'm late. Misty can be a bit slow at times," Melissa greeted them.

"Oh, Mel! What a gorgeous dog!" Jade exclaimed. Excited, Misty strained at her lead to reach Jade, tail wagging. Melissa struggled to hold the dog back. She was worried that Misty would jump up.

"Shall we grab an ice-cream and head down to the beach first?" she suggested. "Misty loves swimming."

The three girls walked along the waterfront to *Amo Gelato* and queued up for ice-creams. They all checked their phones while they waited. After a few moments, Melissa looked up and saw a boy rollerblading down the promenade towards them.

Her heart started to beat hard.

It's Josh.

She stared as he drew closer, but when the rollerblader looked up, she realised he wasn't the good-looking boy from school, after all.

Melissa glanced away. Her face started to feel warm.

I don't know why you get so nervous. He doesn't even talk to you.

It was true. Josh didn't bully her – but he wasn't her friend.

Luckily, Jade and Amira didn't notice her embarrassment. They were still looking at their phones.

"Next, please," the ice-cream seller called out.

They ate their ice-creams by the sea, while the dog barked and danced in the water. Misty came out of the sea sometimes to make sure they were still there and to shake water all over them, before running back into the waves.

"Misty, get away!" they all shouted.

It was nearly 1pm when they went back up to the promenade. The restaurants were very busy now. It was the first sunny day in a while, and many Londoners travelled down to Brighton to enjoy a day at the beach.

As they walked along the promenade, they passed a sign. Melissa stopped to read it.

Brighton Seafront 10 km Fun Run

Saturday 24 September. Start time: 10am.

All welcome. Prizes for the winners and best costume.

"What do you think?" asked Melissa, turning to her friends. "We could enter together?"

"Nah," Jade replied, pulling a face.

"Boring," Amira added.

Melissa forced a smile. "Oh ... just kidding," she replied, pretending it didn't matter. Amira and Jade were her new – and only – friends here, and she wanted to fit in with them. "Fun runs are for losers."

"Hi there," a voice called out from behind them. "What are you guys up to?"

The group turned around, to find Andy, from school, standing behind them. He was on his own and wore a friendly smile.

"Oh, hi," Jade replied. She didn't sound so friendly.
"We spent the morning on the beach," Melissa said. She noted then, how Jade and Amira looked at each other.
"We're just off home," Jade said.
"Yeah," Amira added. "My dad's picking me up in a few minutes."
Melissa frowned. They were making excuses. They didn't have to go home now. Instead, they were going to the city centre and planned to walk through the Lanes next to do some window shopping.
Andy's face fell.
Melissa felt bad for him. And yet she remained silent.
"Okay." Andy gave a small smile. "I guess I'll see you in class tomorrow."
The girls said goodbye and continued east along the promenade. When Andy was far behind them, Jade turned to Melissa and smiled. "We certainly don't need *him* hanging around with us."

COMPREHENSION QUESTIONS

1. What happened at school on Wednesday?
2. What is visible from miles around?
3. Who did Melissa think she saw rollerblading on the promenade?

DISCUSSION QUESTIONS

1. Jade and Amira are unfriendly to Andy. Melissa doesn't say anything, even though she isn't happy with their behaviour. What would you do in this situation?
2. Melissa hopes Jade and Amira will join her in the fun run, but they are not interested. To fit in, Melissa then pretends that she is not interested either. What would you do in this situation?

Chapter Four: The Game

PRE-READING VOCABULARY EXERCISE

Match the words (1-13) with their definitions (a-m):

1. shoved	a. look closely at
2. back and forth	b. amusing, funny
3. groaned	c. type of biscuit
4. surveyed	d. move back and forth, sway
5. frowning	e. disaster
6. catastrophe	f. romantic comedy movie
7. laughable	g. disappoint everyone
8. dumb	h. push roughly
9. let everyone down	i. move quickly
10. hurried/racing	j. explanation to justify behaviour
11. shortbread	k. stupid
12. rom-com	l. furrow the brow to show disapproval
13. excuse	m. a deep sound to show despair

CHAPTER SUMMARY

There's a football match at school. Melissa is chosen for Josh's team. He starts talking to her in the break, but someone interrupts him. Melissa scores an own goal, and the other students are unkind to her. Even her friends Jade and Amira don't support her. Afterwards Jade and Amira invite her to join them at Jade's house. Melissa declines because she is not impressed by the two girls' behaviour.

"James, if I see that phone again, I'll take it off you for the rest of the week," shouted out Mr O'Reilly, the PE teacher. James hurriedly shoved his phone back in his pocket. "Sorry, Sir."

It was early afternoon, and the class walked over to the football field behind the school. Melissa, Jade, and Amira chatted at the back of the group.

Melissa was relieved to get out of the classroom, but she wasn't sure the other students would leave her alone. Out front, kicking the ball back and forth between them, and making a lot of noise, were Josh and his friends.

By the time the three girls reached the field, the others were already standing around talking excitedly or taking turns kicking the ball into the net.

"Look, everyone, Beetroot Girl's here!" yelled a boy about to take a shot at goal.

Melissa looked down at the ground and blushed, while many students laughed.

"Hey look ... she's turning red again!" Someone called out.

"All right, let's have a bit of healthy competition," said Mr O'Reilly.

Melissa frowned. She loved to go running with Misty, but team sports weren't fun for her. She didn't like how aggressive some people became.

"I'm going to divide you into teams now," declared Mr O'Reilly. "Jennifer – you're captain of Team A, Josh – you're captain of Team B, now—"

"Sir, can we choose our own teams?" Josh asked.

Mr O'Reilly smiled. "You'd like that wouldn't you, Josh? And that's why *I'm* going to pick the teams." He then surveyed the students around him. "Ayesha – Team A, Amira – Team B, Melissa ... which team will we put you on?"

The answer was Team B – with Josh. Some of the other students groaned when Mr O'Reilly placed her on their team.

Josh surveyed his players. Of course, he had a few friends with him. But Melissa wasn't one of them.

Melissa's face grew hot again. She wanted to get to know Josh better, and this was her chance. But she didn't know what to say, and so she stayed silent.

Josh assigned positions to everyone, before turning to her. He then gave her a big smile. "Okay, Melissa ... how do you feel about playing defender?"

Melissa stared into his eyes and nodded.

"You can play, can't you?" A girl on her team asked, frowning.

"Yeah ... sure," she replied, as her face got hotter.

The teams were chosen, positions assigned, and the players spread out on the field. Melissa took up position on the left of the goalie. Amira had been chosen to play defender too and stood on the right of the posts.

Mr O'Reilly blew the whistle, and the game started.

"Melissa!"

She glanced up to see the ball racing towards her – followed by a boy and a girl charging in her direction.

"Melissa!" came the shout again. "Pass the ball over here."

She gave the ball a good kick when it reached her. Much to everyone's relief, and her amazement, the ball travelled directly to Holly, who then rushed off down the field with it, taking everyone with her.

Phew! Catastrophe averted. Pressure off. Melissa was then able to relax once more.

The game continued. Team B was strong, and Melissa spent most of the game watching the play. Josh called out to his friends at the far end of the field. Suddenly, there was great excitement, and cries went up as Josh scored for their team. After that, Mr O'Reilly blew the whistle for half time.

Melissa joined the rest of her team while they discussed tactics. Then, Josh moved close to Melissa and met her eye. "Well done," he said with a smile. "Mel, do you—"

"Hey, Josh. I've got a strategy for the second half," one of the boys, Jake, called out.

Turning away, Josh focused on the game once more.

Melissa was disappointed by the interruption. *What was he going to ask me?*

After fifteen minutes, they swapped sides and were back on the field again.

The game continued, but eventually Melissa got bored. She hoped the game would finish soon so she could go home.

But then she saw the ball coming her way again. Ayesha, from the opposing team, ran down the pitch, kicking the ball ahead of her. Players on Melissa's team were converging on the approaching attacker, when Ayesha lost control of the ball and it shot towards Melissa.

"Quickly, pass it here," called out their goalie. Panicking, Melissa deflected the ball towards the goal posts. But she swung her foot too hard.

The ball lifted off the ground and landed in the middle of the net.

"I said PASS it," shouted the goalkeeper as he fell to his knees.

The looks of shock and horror on her teammates' faces were almost laughable—but the abuse that followed was not.

"What's wrong with you, Beetroot Girl?"

She stared down at the ground.

"How could you be so dumb?"

"You idiot ... you've just cost us the win."

Melissa looked up again then as she recognised the voice. She stared into Josh's angry, red face.

She'd let everyone down.

"Hey Mel, wait up!"

Jade and Amira caught up with Melissa as she hurried towards the school gate. "Do you want to come around to my place again tonight?" asked Jade. "We're going to do some baking and watch a movie."

Melissa turned and looked at the girls. She was hurt her new friends didn't defend her on the football field. *No one* defended her. "No, thanks, I'm good," she replied after a pause.

"You're okay, aren't you?" asked Amira. "I mean, everyone was just disappointed. They don't hate you."

"Yeah, I'm fine."

She wasn't, actually.

"But you *must* come," Jade insisted. "It'll be lots of fun. The three of us. We're going to make shortbread."

"Yeah, you have to come," said Amira. "We'll watch a rom-com afterwards."

"I can't ... I'm helping my parents at home."

It wasn't a good excuse, but she couldn't think of anything else.

"Oh, okay," said Jade, frowning. "Maybe next time."

COMPREHENSION QUESTIONS

1. Why doesn't Melissa like team sports?

2. Why does it really hurt that Josh, especially, is unkind after she scores an own goal?

3. What did Jade and Amira invite Melissa around to do?

DISCUSSION QUESTIONS

1. Melissa's new friends want her to do all the things they do and aren't always supportive of her. She is starting to question the friendship. What do you think makes a good friendship?

2. Melissa doesn't like team sports. Why do you think it is difficult for someone who's shy to play team sports?

Chapter Five: Reflections in the Park

PRE-READING VOCABULARY EXERCISE

Match the words (1-11) with their definitions (a-k):

1. casserole	a. clothing
2. wafted	b. a community within a town or city
3. peeled	c. town and seaside resort in England
4. gear	d. pass gently through the air
5. whistled	e. indicate with your hand
6. bark	f. the noise a dog makes
7. neighbourhood	g. a stew cooked slowly in the oven
8. sped off	h. make a high-pitched sound by forcing air between the lips and teeth
9. chased	i. pursued or followed aggressively
10. gesturing	j. leave very quickly (past)
11. Blackpool	k. with the outer skin removed

CHAPTER SUMMARY

Melissa is still unhappy at her new school and doesn't know what to do. She wants to try and fix the problem herself. Melissa and Misty go for a run to the park. She meets Andy and his sister there. She learns that Andy's life has been hard lately. She is impressed by how he deals with life and feels inspired to make changes to her own.

"What's wrong, Mel?" her mother asked.

They sat in the kitchen. The smell of chicken casserole wafted through the house. Melissa's mum worked on an apple pie for dessert at the kitchen table. She peeled the apples while her daughter sat silently staring out the window.

Melissa usually loved her mum's cooking, but even the delicious aroma of the casserole couldn't cheer her up this afternoon.

"Nothing."

Of course, that was a lie. What was she going to do about school?

She should talk to her mum. And she would, if things didn't improve. But she wanted to try and sort things out for herself first.

However, her mum wasn't giving up. "You've hardly said a word since you came home from school ... that's not like you."

"I've got a headache." Another lie. "I'm going for a run with Misty ... maybe that will help."

She went upstairs to change into her running gear. When she came back down, she grabbed the dog lead and whistled for Misty.

Her mother was putting the pie in the oven. She looked around as her daughter entered the kitchen and frowned. "Are you still having problems at school, love?"

Melissa shook her head.

"What are Amira and Jade up to today?"

"Don't know," Melissa replied. "Come on, Misty."

She felt bad about being dishonest with her mum, but she needed some time alone this afternoon.

A run would make her feel better. It always did.

And spending time with Misty made everything all right.

The park was only a couple of blocks from their home. When they reached the large sports field, she let Misty off the lead. The dog gave a loud bark and ran off while Melissa continued running around the edge of the park.

School was bad, but she liked having the park and the beach nearby – things that had been missing in their old neighbourhood back in Birmingham. Misty loved these places too.

"Arf! Arf!" The dog sped off down the football pitch to where a boy and a girl were kicking a ball.

Melissa gasped. *Oh no! She's going to steal their ball.* "Misty! Misty!"

She chased her dog, but it was too late. Misty reached the pair then and barked enthusiastically while she waited for them to kick the ball again. Melissa was out of breath by the time she caught up with her dog.

"I'm so sorry! I really—"

Melissa stopped talking. She knew the boy, from school.

It was Andy.

Her face turned warm.

Great, Beetroot Girl is back.

She felt bad about Andy. In class, she was always relieved when the bullies focused on him, rather than her. But that wasn't fair. She was also embarrassed about how rude Amira and Jade were to him on the promenade. He didn't deserve that either.

Andy smiled at her. "That's okay," he replied before pausing. "This is my little sister, Laura, by the way," he said, gesturing towards the young girl who was with him. "We live just around the corner from here."

"I live close by too," said Melissa. This was her first conversation with Andy. At school, no one talked to him – so she didn't either. "I'm an only child. Do you have other brothers and sisters?"

"One elder brother," he replied with a shy smile. "Mum died a year ago, so dad has to look after us on his own."

"That must be hard for him ... and for you all."

Andy shrugged. "Dad says we don't have much money, but he's saving to take us all to Blackpool at Christmas."

"That's great," Melissa replied. "I love Blackpool!"

She was surprised Andy looked so happy – even though he was bullied every day at school. He was stronger than he appeared. Melissa didn't like Beal High, but she was lucky. She still had her mum, and her family didn't worry about money.

"Well, sorry again about my dog." She stepped back, about to continue her run. "She gets too excited sometimes."

She was just about to go, when Andy spoke. “We’re only kicking the ball around. But you can join us, if you’d like? It’s better with more people.”

Melissa smiled. “Sounds good.” She paused then. “But I’m warning you, I’m not very good at football.”

Andy grinned. “I know.” Of course, he was on the football field today. “But you just need practice, that’s all.”

COMPREHENSION QUESTIONS

1. What was Melissa’s mum making for dessert?

2. Who was Andy with at the park?

3. What reason does Andy give for inviting Melissa to kick the ball with them?

DISCUSSION QUESTIONS

1. Melissa’s mother tries to talk to her about her problems at school, but Melissa doesn’t want to talk about them. If you had problems at school, would you talk to your parents about them? Why or why not?

2. Melissa is impressed by Andy because, despite the difficulties in his life and the bullying he suffers, he manages to remain positive. Think of someone in your own life who impresses you by their behaviour. Why do they impress you? What could you learn from them?

Chapter Six: Gobsmacked

PRE-READING VOCABULARY EXERCISE

Match the words (1-15) with their definitions (a-o):

1. quiz	a. hair growth on chin and lower cheeks
2. site	b. serve with a large spoon
3. blurted out	c. hall at school where students eat lunch
4. escape	d. area
5. glared	e. get in a line behind others
6. fit in	f. very shocked, astonished
7. beard	g. flat, shallow container for carrying food plates on
8. dinner hall	h. food crushed to a soft mass
9. queue	i. exclaim, say something abruptly
10. mash	j. large sheet of paper used to advertise something
11. ladled	k. flat cake of batter, fried on both sides
12. tray	l. socially compatible with a group
13. stunned/gobsmacked	m. get away from control
14. pancakes	n. stare in an angry way
15. poster	o. test of knowledge

CHAPTER SUMMARY

There's a quiz in history class. Melissa answers many questions and begins to grow in confidence. She realises she is no longer blushing. She is enjoying herself and doesn't care what others think of her. Melissa declines to go out with Josh. She surprises Jade and Amira by telling them she will be in the fun run.

"All right, class," said Mr Jones, "We're going to end today with a quiz on English kings and queens. Laptops closed, please."

Melissa liked Mr Jones. He was softly spoken and had the ability to bring history to life. Besides, this was her favourite subject.

Like her mum, Melissa had a passion for English history.

"Okay, class, Question One," called out Mr Jones. "Who became king after the Battle of Hastings in 1066?"

Too easy, thought Melissa, recalling her family's holiday to the coast a few years earlier. They visited the site of the battle between the Anglo Saxons and the Normans.

"Well?" called out Mr Jones. "Surely, somebody has an idea? It's only just up the road from here."

Everyone looked blank as Mr Jones walked around the room, hands behind his back.

"William the Conqueror," blurted out Melissa.

"Well done, Melissa." Mr Jones nodded, pleased to have received a response from one of his students.

Around Melissa, other students turned and looked in her direction.

"Question Two, then." continued Mr Jones. "Who was the first King of England, Scotland and Ireland?"

Melissa knew this one too. When she was eleven, her family went on a trip up to Scotland for a couple of weeks.

Again, there was a long pause. "Err ... James II?" offered a girl from the back of the room.

"Almost," said Mr Jones.

"James I," Melissa called out.

"Correct, Melissa. Quite the history expert, aren't you?"

Glancing around, she saw that some students appeared relieved to escape the teacher's attention. However, a few of them glared at her.

It seemed she couldn't do anything right.

But this time, Melissa stared back at them.

And this time, she didn't go red.

She loved history, and she wasn't going to pretend she was stupid just to fit in.

The quiz continued, and Mr Jones's questions got harder and harder. One or two other students answered, but mostly Melissa replied. She was really enjoying herself.

"Final question, then," Mr Jones said with a grin, glancing at his watch. "Who was the last king to have a beard?"

That was a difficult one.

She had a good memory for faces, and her mother had lots of books about the English kings. But which ones had beards?

George VI didn't have one, and neither did Edward VIII.

She didn't like beards – and certainly wouldn't like a boyfriend with one!

"George V, Sir," she shouted out.

Everyone was now staring at her, but she didn't care.

Melissa was smiling as she walked into the dinner hall.

What a great quiz! But best of all, she felt confident. She had nothing to prove to the other students – only to herself.

Melissa joined the dinner queue. She then wrinkled her nose at the smell.

What have they done to the poor vegetables today?

"What would you like, love?" the dinner lady asked Melissa. "We've got a choice of sausages or meatballs, and hash browns, carrot mash ... and mushy peas. Oh, and ice-cream and jelly or apple pie for dessert."

"I'll have the sausages, and ice-cream and jelly, thanks."

Melissa watched as the woman ladled a big serving of lumpy carrot mash onto her plate. "There you go, love. Enjoy!"

Melissa took her tray and walked towards the tables. It was crowded and noisy in the dinner hall. She was busy looking for a seat when a boy stepped up next to her. "Hey, Melissa!"

Josh. He was carrying a tray with a big plate of meatballs and hash browns.

"Look, there's Beetroot Girl," Liam called out from a nearby table.

"What a loser," James shouted. "Scored more own goals recently?"

Liam and James laughed then, but Josh didn't. Instead, he turned to Melissa. "I'm sorry about the football game. I didn't mean to shout at you." He paused then, embarrassed. "Are you free on Friday, after school? We can go to the movies?"

Melissa couldn't believe Josh was asking her out. He was good-looking and popular too. But she wasn't interested in him anymore.

"Why are you talking to *her*, Josh?" James shouted.

Melissa ignored him. Instead, she smiled at Josh. "Thanks for the apology, but I'm busy on Friday." She glanced to where Liam and James sat smirking. "You should really find some better friends."

Josh looked stunned, but he didn't say anything.

Still smiling, Melissa continued towards the back of the hall. Ahead, she saw Jade and Amira eating lunch together. She joined them at their table.

"Mel. You were great in class today," Amira said.

"Yeah," agreed Jade. "Hey, do you want to join us for pancakes at my house on Saturday morning?"

Melissa liked her new friends, but she had other plans for Saturday. "I can't ... not this weekend. I've entered that fun run – the one we saw the poster for. I have to be down on the seafront by 9.30am."

"You did?" Jade asked.

"Oh," Amira replied.

The pair of them wore gobsmacked expressions.

COMPREHENSION QUESTIONS

1. How does Melissa know the answer to the teacher's question about the Battle of Hastings?

2. What would Melissa not want a boyfriend to have?

3. What was Josh having for lunch?

DISCUSSION QUESTIONS

1. Melissa finds her self-confidence improving in history class. Do you think students are less likely to bully a confident student? Why or why not?

2. Josh asks Melissa out, but she turns him down because of his friends and the way he treated her at the game. Would you go out with someone who didn't treat you well, or had friends who didn't treat you well? Why or why not?

Chapter Seven: A Real Winner

PRE-READING VOCABULARY EXERCISE

Match the words (1-22) with their definitions (a-v):

1. gathered	a. small insect
2. entrants	b. nervous feeling
3. rammed	c. gentle wind
4. bugs	d. people out front
5. glistening	e. person who watches an event
6. breeze	f. mental state that allows a person to perform at the best of their ability
7. megaphone	g. walk/run with difficulty due to injury
8. spectators	h. move at a particular speed
9. butterflies in the stomach	i. rub against a hard surface
10. pace	j. wobbly, shaky on the feet
11. pavement	k. meet together
12. sweat	l. squeeze tightly
13. pull away	m. device for amplifying the voice
14. leaders	n. leave quickly
15. in the zone	o. long seat for many people
16. scraped	p. person who takes part in something
17. bench	q. heading at the top of the page in a newspaper
18. unsteady	r. shine with a sparkling light
19. limping	s. move off ahead
20. took off	t. very crowded
21. headline	u. moisture on skin from physical exertion
22. hugged	v. area for pedestrians at side of the road

CHAPTER SUMMARY

Melissa and Misty line up for the start of the fun run. Jade and Amira are there to support her. She tries to stay with the quickest runners. Melissa reflects on what she has learned since moving to Brighton. The race is going well, when she sees Andy. Andy falls and hurts himself, and Melissa goes to help him. He continues the race, and she supports him to the end. Melissa and Andy appear on the front page of the local newspaper.

Melissa and Misty gathered with the other entrants for the start of the race.

The seafront was rammed with runners and their supporters. There was a real mix of people there. Some were doing warm-up exercises, while others were standing around impatiently waiting for the race to begin. Some were dressed as giant penguins and bugs, while others wore very serious, focused expressions.

"Not long now, Misty," Melissa said, as she bent down to give the dog a pat on the head. "I hope you aren't as nervous as me."

Misty just wagged her tail. She clearly wasn't.

Melissa tried to relax. She was full of nervous energy. She'd always wanted to take part in something like this. She'd just lacked the courage to do it on her own.

The seafront was the ideal place for a fun run. It was a flat, vibrant area. The sun was glistening off the sea this morning, and there was a soft breeze.

"Good morning, everyone," a man called out at the front through a megaphone. "It's great to have you all here for the inaugural Brighton Seafront Fun Run."

A cheer went up from the surrounding spectators.

Butterflies danced in Melissa's stomach.

"Go, Mel!"

Melissa saw Jade and Amira in the crowd. Smiling, she waved back. It felt good to have the support of her new friends.

"To complete the run, make sure you go around the turn at the other end of the seafront," the man with the megaphone continued. "Good luck!" He then sounded the horn for the start of the race.

"Arf! Arf!" The excitement was too much for Misty. Melissa and the dog took off at a steady pace, trying to navigate their way through the crowd towards the front. She didn't want to go too hard early on, but she needed to stay with the first group of runners.

As the front group pulled away, she enjoyed the feel of the pavement under her feet and the sun on her face. Misty was trotting along comfortably beside her. Melissa was in her happy place.

Maybe Brighton wasn't so bad, after all.

She had friends, and there were plenty of new places for her and Misty to explore together.

Melissa began to run a little faster then, as the group sped up. She was breathing hard now and starting to sweat.

School had been difficult at times. The bullying wasn't nice, but things were getting better. She felt stronger, happier.

She appreciated her mum's support, but she didn't need her to contact the school principal, after all.

She enjoyed Jade and Amira's company, but she didn't need to hang around with them all the time, and behave like them.

She liked Josh, but she didn't need a cute, popular guy as a boyfriend – especially one who was friends with bullies.

She understood now. If she wanted to be happy, in life and at school, she just needed to be herself. She had to be proud of who she was. Even when she blushed.

"Arf! Arf!" Misty barked again.

Melissa noticed that the group was starting to break up. The front runners were pulling away, while others were starting to fall back towards the main group. Melissa decided to chase the leaders.

Her legs were starting to feel tired as she turned the corner at the end of the seafront and headed back towards town and the finish line. Even Misty was panting now.

But Melissa was happy. She was really in the zone. Just her, Misty, and the sound of her feet hitting the pavement. She grabbed another drink, from a table along the route, and gulped it down. The first runners were far ahead now, but she was still doing really well. Those around her looked much older than her.

"Come on, Misty," she panted. "We can do it!"

And then she saw him.

Andy was running towards her in the opposite direction.

Melissa grinned. *I didn't know he was running today!*

But a moment later, Andy tripped on the pavement and fell on his face.

Melissa stopped.

The race forgotten, she ran to her friend. "Andy, are you okay?"

He nodded and got to his feet. His hands and knees were badly scraped, and there was a cut on his left cheek.

Spectators looked on in concern.

"Let's sit down on this bench over here," Melissa suggested.

Andy shook his head. "I want to continue the race."

Melissa wasn't sure that was a great idea. His injuries weren't serious, but he really should get them cleaned.

But Andy wouldn't give up. He started running again. He looked a bit unsteady at first. He was limping, obviously still in pain.

Melissa watched him go, unsure what to do.

She was out of the race now, but that wasn't important. What mattered was that Andy was okay. She was impressed he wasn't giving up.

Melissa looked down at her dog. "Ready, Misty? We can't let him run the rest of the race alone."

A moment later, they took off after Andy.

Local Girl Helps Injured Boy Finish Race.

Melissa read the <u>headline</u> and looked at the accompanying photo in the Brighton Times.

She and Andy had made the front page.

"Well done, Mel," said her father from across the kitchen table. The family were having breakfast together. "We'll have to buy extra copies of the newspaper to send to all the relatives."

"The front page, Mel!" Her mother <u>hugged</u> her. "This calls for a full English breakfast to celebrate!"

"That sounds great, mum ... thanks!" Melissa glanced back down at the picture of her and Andy on the seafront. They were both holding up their finishing certificates. Melissa smiled. "I think I'm going to like it here, after all," she announced.

"I am pleased to hear that," her mum replied. "Andy looks like a nice boy. Why don't you ask him around for dinner, Mel?"

And with that, Melissa went bright red.

The End

COMPREHENSION QUESTIONS

1. What were some people 'in costume' dressed as?

2. What injuries did Andy have as a result of his fall?

3. Why does Melissa's father want to buy extra copies of the newspaper?

DISCUSSION QUESTIONS

1. Melissa gives up her position in the race to help Andy when he is injured. Would you help Andy in this situation or race to the finish line?

2. Melissa shows that the best way to be happy in life is to find your own inner strength, to live life your way and not rely too much on others or worry about what they think. Why do you think it is important not to worry too much about what others think of you?

Answer key

Chapter One

1. g, 2. j. 3. a, 4. k, 5. d, 6. l, 7. m, 8. b, 9. c, 10. e, 11. i, 12. h, 13. f

Comprehension

1. She doesn't want to be asked a question.
2. He kicks her chair.
3. She tells them to come and see her after class.

Chapter Two

1. o, 2. i, 3. j, 4. n, 5. v, 6. s, 7. q, 8. t, 9. a, 10. c, 11. h, 12. d, 13. f, 14. u, 15. e, 16. r, 17. b, 18. l, 19. k, 20. p, 21. m, 22. g

Comprehension

1. Explore the seafront with Misty and take her for a swim.
2. Go for a run.
3. James and Liam are bullying her.

Chapter Three

1. f, 2. i, 3. a, 4. k, 5. b, 6. h, 7. c, 8. e, 9. d, 10. g, 11. j

Comprehension

1. A boy threw her books across the classroom.
2. The Brighton Pole.
3. Josh.

Chapter Four

1. h, 2. d, 3. m, 4. a, 5. l, 6. e, 7. b, 8. k, 9. g, 10. i, 11. c, 12. f, 13. j

Comprehension

1. She doesn't like how aggressive some people become.
2. Because she really likes Josh.
3. Bake shortbread and watch a movie.

Chapter Five

1. g, 2. d, 3. k, 4. a, 5. h, 6. f, 7. b, 8. j, 9. i, 10. e, 11. c

1. Apple pie.
2. His sister.
3. It's better with more people.

Chapter Six

1. o, 2. d, 3. i, 4. m, 5. n, 6. l, 7. a, 8. c, 9. e, 10. h, 11. b, 12. g, 13. f, 14. k, 15. j

Comprehension

1. She visited the site of the battle with her parents a few years earlier.
2. A beard.
3. Meatballs and hashbrowns.

Chapter Seven

1. k, 2. p, 3. t, 4. a, 5. r, 6. c, 7. m, 8. e, 9. b, 10. h, 11. v, 12. u, 13. s, 14. d, 15. f, 16. i, 17. o, 18. j, 19. g, 20. n, 21. q, 22. l

Comprehension

1. Giant penguins and bugs.
2. His hands and knees were badly scraped, and there was a cut on his left cheek.
3. To send to all the relatives.

About the Author

Timothy Burton has a very nice life. He was once lucky enough to have his own gorgeous Bearded Collie. His great hope is that everyone finds their own inner strength.

Have a question?

Get in touch with Timothy Burton at
timothyburtonbooks@gmail.com

Manufactured by Amazon.ca
Acheson, AB